Joyce Dunbar

Lara Jones

I want a mini TIGER

MACMILLAN CHILDREN'S BOOKS

I want a crocodile!
A mini crocodile!

A snappy happy grinny crocodile.

To sit upon my shoulder
and nuzzle at my ear.

You can't have a crocodile!
A mini crocodile.
A snappy happy grinny crocodile.

Crocodiles have sharp teeth
and would gobble you all up.

Besides . . .

A crocodile needs a river.

I want an elephant!
A little elephant!

A trundle rumble tumble elephant.

To sit next to me at teatime

and tickle me with his trunk.

You can't have an elephant!

A little elephant.

A trundle rumble tumble elephant.

An elephant would squash you flat
and squirt you with its trunk.

Besides . . .

An elephant needs the jungle.

I want a monkey!
A funky monkey!

A honky-tonky jumpy monkey.
To catch and chase with me
and curl up very small.

You can't have a monkey!

A funky monkey.

A honky-tonky jumpy monkey.

A monkey would make mischief
and snatch your food away.

Besides . . .

A monkey needs the trees.

I want a **bear!**

A pocket bear!

A grizzly growly gruesome bear.

To peep out of my coat

and show off to my friends.

You can't have a bear!

A pocket bear.

A grizzly growly gruesome bear.

A **real** bear would roar
so loud you'd run
away in fright.

Besides . . .

A bear needs a cave.

You can't have a giraffe!

A small giraffe.

A blinky dinky tame giraffe.

A giraffe would chew your hair
and nibble at your nose.

Besides . . .

A giraffe needs open plains.

I want a tiger!
A mini tiger!

A tiggy taggy togger tiger.

To pounce and prance and
scamper, and snuggle
on my lap.

Can I please have a
tiger,
please?

Here's a tiger!
A mini tiger!
A tiggy taggy togger tiger.

To make everybody laugh.

To show off.

To curl up very small.

To tickle you.

To snuggle on your lap.

To nuzzle your ear.

This tiger is a kitten cat.

And this kitten cat needs . . .